Gray Rabbit's Odd One Out

Alan Baker

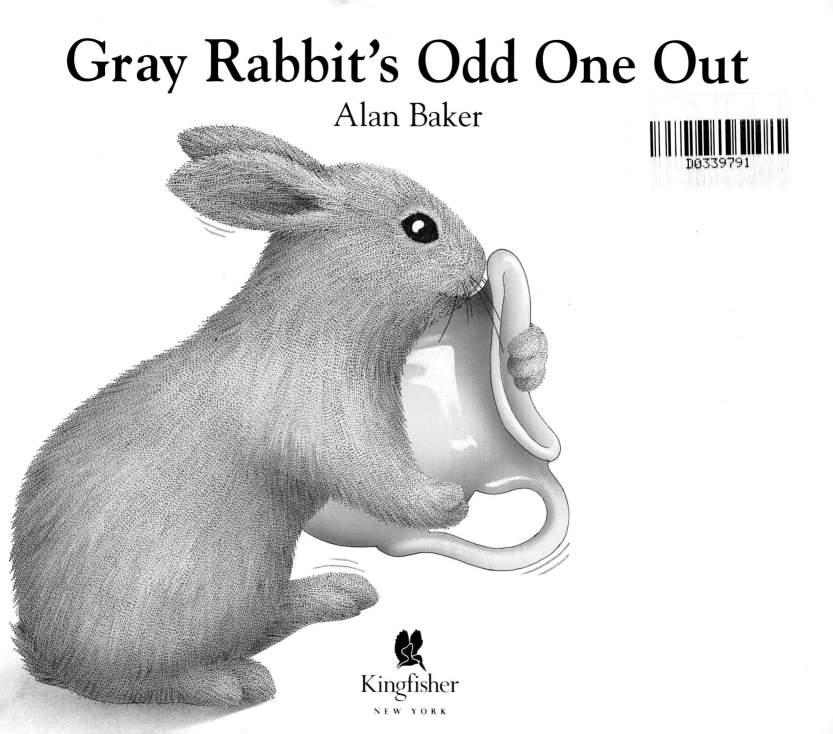

Kingfisher

NEW YORK

KINGFISHER
Larousse Kingfisher Chambers Inc.
95 Madison Avenue
New York, New York 10016

First American edition 1995
2 4 6 8 10 9 7 5 3 1 (HC)
2 4 6 8 10 9 7 5 3 1 (PB)

LIBRARY OF CONGRESS CATALOGING-IN-PUBLICATION DATA
Baker, Alan.
Gray Rabbit's odd one out / Alan Baker.—1st American ed.
p. cm.—(Little rabbit books.)
Summary: Gray rabbit tidies up his room and sorts his belongings
into groups of like things as he searches for his favorite book.
[1. Orderliness—Fiction. 2. Rabbits—Fiction.] I. Title.
II. Series: Baker, Alan. Little rabbit books:
PZ7.B1688Bn 1995
[E]–dc20 94-42002 CIP AC

ISBN 1-85697-585-1 (HC)
ISBN 1-85697-644-0 (PB)

Cover designed by Caroline Johnson
Printed in Singapore

One morning Gray Rabbit could not find his favorite book.

It's time to clean up, thought Rabbit.
First let's sort out the wooden animals.

There were two of each kind—just like in Noah's ark.

But one thing was not an animal.
What was the odd one out?

A teaspoon.

So Rabbit sorted out his cups and saucers.
But one thing did not belong.
What was it?

A paintbrush.

Rabbit gathered up his paints and brushes and made a useful sign. Now what was the odd one out?

A red and yellow polka-dot ball.

Rabbit found all his round things.
Hey, stop rolling away!
But one thing did not belong.
What was it?

A purple vase.
Where can that go? thought Rabbit.
It's the only vase I have.

Then he matched it up with all the other purple things. But something wasn't purple. What was it?

A duck. That belonged with the other stuffed animals, so Rabbit lined them all up in a row.

Now what did not belong?

A block.

There were lots and lots of blocks.
How could Rabbit sort them out?

First he built a square
of red blocks,

then a wall
of green blocks.

The yellow blocks made a tower.
What was that among the blue blocks?

Look! Rabbit's favorite book.
I'll sort out the blue blocks,
he thought, then I'll read
my story.

At last!